In loving memory of Tom and Gerry.

–Davide

For Emma and Pardo.

–Anna

Text copyright © 2018 by Davide Cali.
Illustrations copyright © 2018 by Anna Pirolli.

Library of Congress Cataloging-in-Publication Data available.

ISBN 978-1-4521-6595-0

Manufactured in China.

Design by Alice Seiler.
Typeset in Bodoni Classic Hand.

10 9 8 7 6 5 4 3 2 1

Chronicle Books LLC
680 Second Street
San Francisco, California 94107

Chronicle Books—we see things differently.
Become part of our community at www.chroniclekids.com.

I Hate
My Cats
(A Love Story)

Davide Cali   Anna Pirolli

chronicle books · san francisco

Ginger is the weird one.

She plays with peas,

purrs at artichokes,

and speaks to pigeons.

She likes mint

and chicken
(but only the neighbor's chicken).

Shoes amuse her . . .

especially MY shoes.

And she only drinks
water from the sink.

Sometimes, if she feels like it,

she leaves me little
presents on the floor.

Fred is the lazy one.
He sleeps most of the time . . .

on sweaters

(preferably white ones).

When he isn't sleeping, he likes to rest . . .
on towels (obviously white ones).

Or in the sink.

We share the covers

and the newspaper.

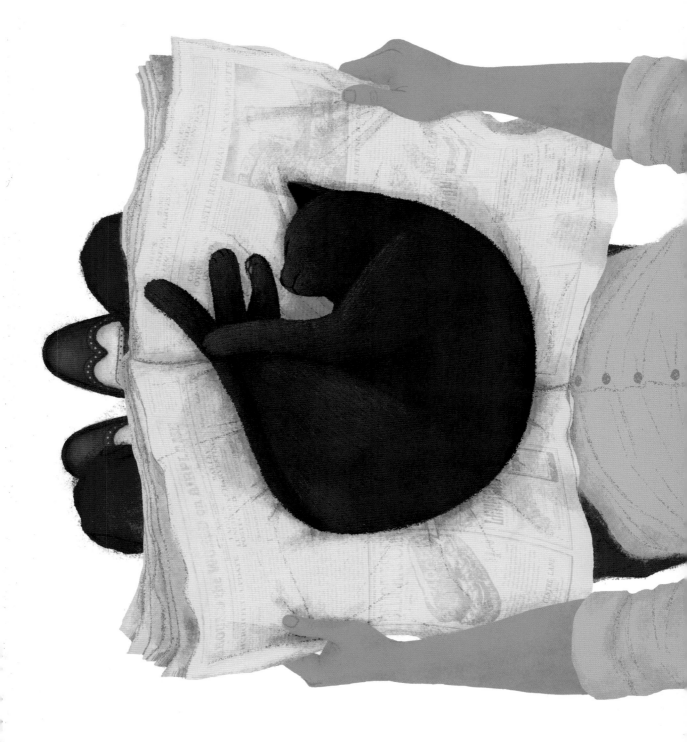

He is friends
with the vase,

and the
side table,

but NOT the
vacuum cleaner.

He disappears whenever I turn it on.

He thinks he's good at hiding . . .

and that nobody can see him.

Sometimes he plays tricks on me.

It's just not fair!

When I can't take it anymore,
I yell, "Stop it!"

By evening, I leave treats
in their bowls to apologize.

FRED

GINGER

But when I go to sleep,
they still haven't appeared.

Then I turn off the light.

In the dark, I feel something move—
something heavy.

They've forgiven me.

Oh, how I hate them!